WITHDRAWN

I Am a Backhoe

Anna Grossnickle Hines

Tricycle Press

Berkeley

Published in the United States by Tricycle Press, an imprint of the
Crown Publishing Group, a division of Random House, Inc., New York.
www.crownpublishing.com
www.tricyclepress.com

Tricycle Press and the Tricycle Press colophon are
registered trademarks of Random House, Inc.

Library of Congress Cataloging-in-Publication Data
Hines, Anna Grossnickle.
I am a backhoe / by Anna Grossnickle Hines.
p. cm.
Summary: A young boy imagines himself to be different
types of trucks as he plays in the sand.
[1. Trucks-Fiction. 2. Play-Fiction.] I. Title.
PZ7.H572Iae 2010
[E]-dc22
2009007534

ISBN 978-1-58246-306-3

Printed in Malaysia
Design by Chloe Rawlins
The illustrations in this book were created digitally.
Typeset in Memphis.
10 9 8 7 6 5 4 3 2 1
First Edition

To Kolbe

I dig my hand
into the sand,
my scooper hand.

Dig. Dig. Dig.
Lift, turn, tip.

I am . . .

a backhoe.

Down on my knees,
I make my hands
into a blade.

Scrape. Push. Plow.
I make a pile.

I am . . .

a bulldozer.

I stretch my arms
into the sky,
way up high.

Bend, hook, lift.
Swooooshhhh.
Swing. Drop.

I am . . .

a crane truck.

I need a big load.
Fill me up.
Now I back up.

Beep, beep, beep.
Tilt and dump.

I am . . .

a dump truck.

Over and over
I roll along.
Smash the ground.

Press it down,
nice and smooth.

I am . . .

a roller.

Daddy puts me
on his back,
his nice flat back.

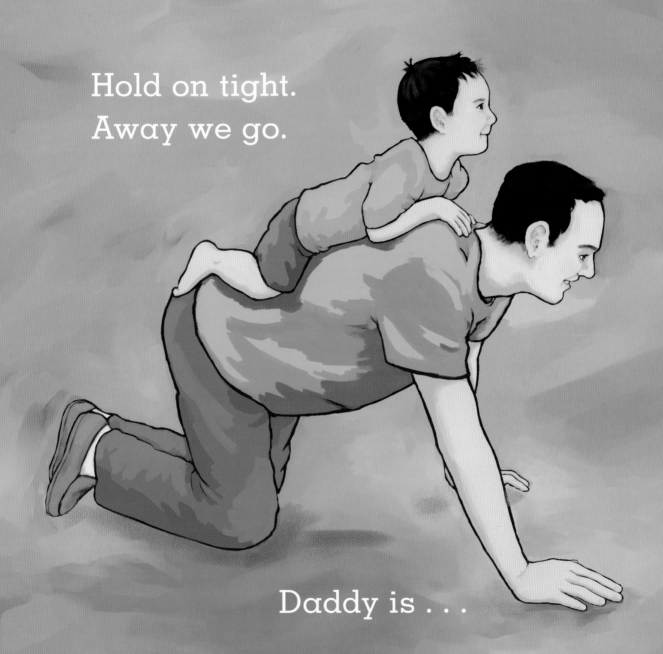

Hold on tight.
Away we go.

Daddy is . . .

a flatbed truck.

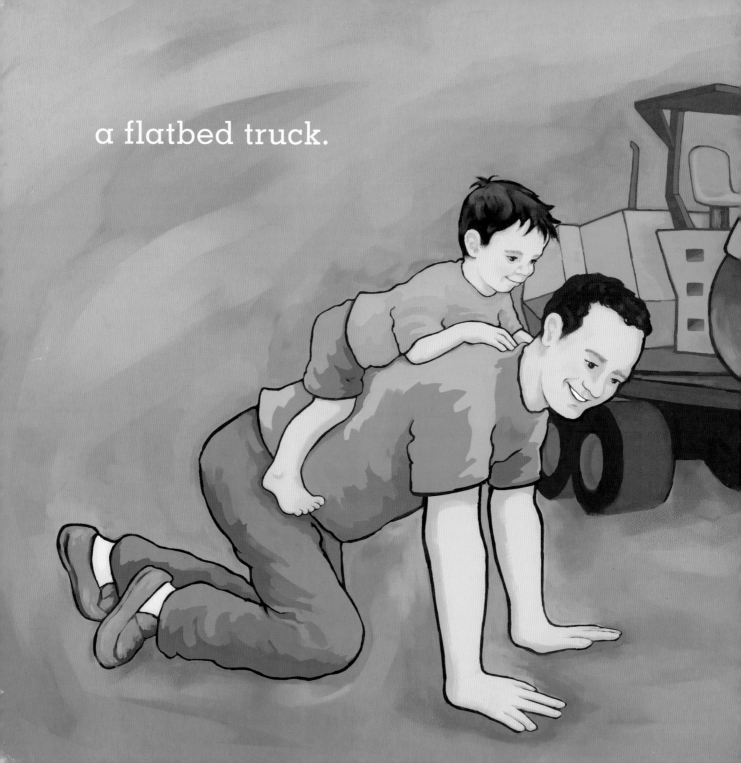

He backs me into
the big garage.
Beep. Beep.
I find my book.

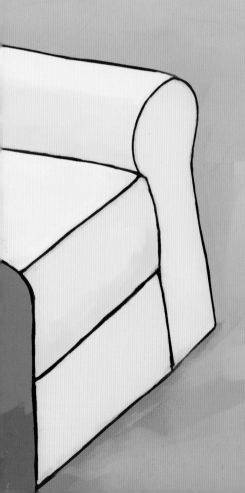

Daddy reads,

"Dig, dig, dig.
Scrape, push, plow.
Bend, hook, lift.
Tilt and dump.
Roll, roll, roll."

I like trucks.